Katie Morag
and Castle McColl

KATIE MORAG AND CASTLE MCCOLL
A RED FOX BOOK 978 1 782 95622 8

First published in Great Britain by The Bodley Head,
an imprint of Random House Children's Publishers UK
A Penguin Random House Company

1 3 5 7 9 10 8 6 4 2

Castle McColl was first published in The Second Katie Morag Storybook
The Bodley Head edition published 1998
Red Fox edition published 2000
This Red Fox edition published 2015

Copyright © Mairi Hedderwick, 1998

Red Fox Books are published by Random House Children's Publishers UK,
61–63 Uxbridge Road, London W5 5SA

www.randomhousechildrens.co.uk
www.randomhouse.co.uk

Addresses for companies within The Random House Group Limited can be found at:
www.randomhouse.co.uk/offices.htm

THE RANDOM HOUSE GROUP Limited Reg. No. 954009

A CIP catalogue record for this book is available from the British Library.

Printed in China

Penguin Random House is committed to a sustainable future for our business, our readers and our planet.
This book is made from Forest Stewardship Council® certified paper.

Katie Morag
and Castle McColl

Mairi Hedderwick

RED FOX

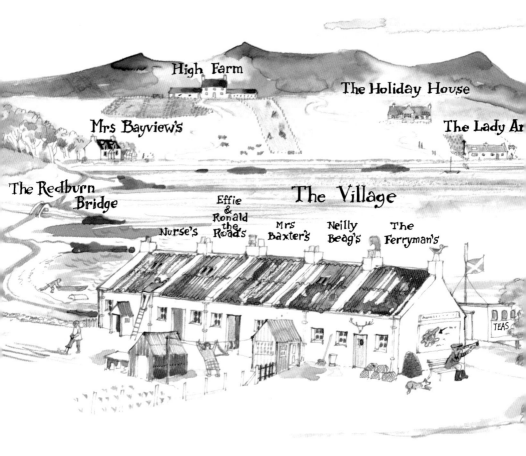

High Farm

The Holiday House

Mrs Bayview's

The Lady Ar

The Redburn
Bridge

The Village

Effie
&
Ronald
the
Road's

Nurse's

Mrs
Baxter's

Neilly
Beag's

The
Ferryman's

TEAS

THE ISLE of STRUAY

rannie's

The Mainland

The New Pier

The Jetty

OBAN TIMES GET YOUR COPY HERE

ISLE of STRUAY SHOP of POST OFFICE

BISTRO

TO THE NEW PIER

CRAFTS

WELCOME

WEST HIGHLAND FREE PRESS

ORDER NOW

LITTE

The Shop & Post Office

Katie Morag McColl's two cats spend most of their time sleeping and stretching, comfy and cuddly on the top of Katie Morag's bed. When the moon is full, however, they go wandering. For days and nights. No one knows where they go. They like it that way. Eventually, with the aid of the great full moon they find their way home.

Fabbydoo is large and a golden gingery red colour. Mr Mistake is smaller and pure white all over. He has one poor eye that can't see a thing but Fabbydoo looks after him. They are great friends.

But not with the Big Boy Cousins. When the Big Boy Cousins come for their holidays to the island they tease Fabbydoo and Mr Mistake. The cats jump off the cosy cushions and hope that the moon is full.

"Here they come! Hide! Hide!"
Katie Morag warned Fabbydoo
and Mr Mistake one day. The boat
had arrived with all the holiday
people and there were the cousins
disembarking with their camping gear.

As long as her cats were hiding
safe, Katie Morag loved it when the
Big Boy Cousins came to stay. They
pitched their tent at Grannie Island's
and Katie Morag was allowed to take
her sleeping bag over and camp too.
It was good knowing that Grannie
was nearby – especially in the middle
of the night.

"It's different this time," declared Hector, the biggest Boy Cousin. "We are pitching the tent by the Castle! It's boring over at Grannie Island's."

What Hector really meant was that the usual site was too close to Grannie Island. There she could keep too much of an eye on them. Once Katie Morag and the Big Boy Cousins got together they got up to all sorts of mischief.

"Please can I go? PLEASE!" Katie Morag implored her parents.

Castle McColl was a long way away from the Village. "Oh! All right," said her father. "As long as you promise to tell them about Clan Chief Rory McColl of the Flaming Red Beard and the Wee White One-Eyed Ghost . . ."

The Big Boy Cousins could
have done without Katie Morag
dragging behind and maybe getting
homesick in the middle of the night,
but stories about Clan Chief Rory
McColl and the Wee White One-
Eyed Ghost sounded interesting.

After all, they were McColls,
too . . .

Castle McColl was ancient. Nobody had lived in it for years and years. Just the pigeons, the mice and a bat or two. Long ago it had been a lively place full of chieftains and warriors, maidens, servants and deerhounds. And the Clan Chief Rory of the Flaming Red Beard. And the Wee White One-Eyed Ghost – if Mr McColl was to be believed . . .

It was very exciting to pitch the tent beside such history, said Hector, pompously, as everyone busied themselves setting up camp. Katie Morag helped Jamie gather old timber from the Castle for the fire. He wanted to hear the stories about the Castle straight away.

"No!" said Katie Morag, a bit bossily. "Once we have had our supper and it is time to go to bed. THAT is the time for stories . . ." She enjoyed knowing something the others did not.

"Bedtime stories! Pah!" sneered Hector after they had gorged on sausages and beans, Grannie Island's apple pie and gallons of juice.

Hector was a bit bad-tempered. There hadn't been enough sausages. He was sure some were missing.

"Yeah!" said Archie. "Try catching me going to bed! I'm going to stay up all night!" The cousins cheered and raced off into the empty gloomy Castle, except for Jamie who felt a bit sorry for Katie Morag and stayed behind.

"Come and tell us the stories in HERE, Katie Morag!" the others teased and taunted, through the arrow-slit windows.

Katie Morag wasn't sure about that. Maybe neither was Jamie. They both wished Grannie Island was nearby. It was beginning to get dark. A big cheesy full moon was coming up over the sea. The glow from the campfire was warm and the sleeping bags in the tent were looking so cosy . . .

But she wasn't going to let the Big
Boy Cousins – or Jamie – know she
was frightened.

"Come on!" she said to Jamie
and ran as fast as she could into the
Castle.

The Big Boy Cousins were hiding, calling with echoey voices from shadowy corners, "Yoo Whoo-oo! Katie Morag and Jamie are afraid of Big Chief Flaming Red Beard and the Wee White One-Eyed Ghost! Fearties! Fearties!"

"We are NOT!" shouted back Katie Morag, riled. "Ready or not, we're coming to get you!"

Everything went silent. The Castle was very scary and eerie. The light coming in through the tiny windows was dim . . . Katie Morag and Jamie held hands and crept the long length of the corridor, their other hands feeling the way along the slimy walls.

Suddenly there was a shrieking and yelling and a blubbering from above. Hector, Archie, Dougal and Murdo Iain came stumbling and clattering down the spiral staircase, terrified out of their wits.

"The Beard! The Beard! It's cut off and it's growling!" screamed Hector as he flew past, heading for the entrance to the Castle.

"And the Wee White One-Eyed Ghost is up there too – just staring and staring with its one eye!" yelled Archie.

Just as Katie Morag and Jamie were turning round to flee for their lives as well, Katie Morag heard the growling.

She recognised it.

Letting go of Jamie's tugging hand she found her way up the darkening staircase to the room above. There in a shadowy corner WAS a big gingery red hairy lump of a thing, very like a cut-off beard. And it WAS growling . . .

It was Fabbydoo chewing his way
through a string of sausages!

Fabbydoo always growls when
he is happy. So does Mr Mistake.
So guess who was the Wee White
One-Eyed Ghost staring and staring,
waiting patiently for his share?

"Oh! Fabbydoo and Mr Mistake,
aren't you wonderful!" whispered
Katie Morag, giving them each a
cuddle. "See you back home at the
end of the full moon – and the
camping holiday!" Then she carefully

found her way down the dark stairs and along the even darker corridor to the outside of the Castle. The dark blue sky was full of stars.

The Big Boy Cousins were huddled in their sleeping bags in the tent, still terrified by their experience, amazed at Katie Morag's bravery. She decided not to tell them about Fabbydoo and Mr Mistake.

"Now it's time for bedtime stories," she said.

"No thank you!" replied the Big Boy Cousins, scaredly, and rolled over to sleep.

Katie Morag sat for a while looking out of the tent flap at the moon, the stars and the silhouette of Castle McColl before she snuggled down to sleep. She could hear Mr Mistake's growl . . . Good, she thought, it was his turn now to get a share of the sausages.

Then she thought she might tell Jamie in the morning about the real Flaming Red Beard and the real Wee White One-Eyed Ghost. But only if he could keep the secret . . .

Castle McColl

Castle McColl is an ancient place of ancient stones and ancient bones. Far and away the WORSTEST place — DON'T go in! DON'T GO IN! Through the black dark creaking door there are corridor horrors with fungal balungals and slime slafalime. It's terrible scerrible and slugawful slippery; it's bugawful squashery, and bat-awful squeakery. It's spidery crydery - all in your hair! Hidery! Hidery! There are ghosts whoo-whoo-hooing up the stairs and rats a'rastussing down below!

THE TEAM

TEAM

RUN! RUN

VISITORS' BEDROOM

VISITOR'S LOO

CLAN CHIEF RORY'S BEDROOM

DEERHOUNDS' BEDROOM

RORY'S LOO

MINSTRELS' GALLERY

BANQUETING HALL

KITCHEN

PIT PRISON

ME OUT!

DROWNING STONE WELL

HELP!

THE TEAM

Footprints on the Beach

Someone hasn't been
on the sand — yet!
I wonder who?